Dear Parents:

Congratulations! Your child is taking the first steps on an exciting journey. The destination? Independent reading!

STEP INTO READING® will help your child get there. The program offers five steps to reading success. Each step includes fun stories and colorful art or photographs. In addition to original fiction and books with favorite characters, there are Step into Reading Non-Fiction Readers, Phonics Readers and Boxed Sets, Sticker Readers, and Comic Readers—a complete literacy program with something to interest every child.

Learning to Read, Step by Step!

Ready to Read   Preschool–Kindergarten
• big type and easy words • rhyme and rhythm • picture clues
For children who know the alphabet and are eager to begin reading.

Reading with Help   Preschool–Grade 1
• basic vocabulary • short sentences • simple stories
For children who recognize familiar words and sound out new words with help.

Reading on Your Own   Grades 1–3
• engaging characters • easy-to-follow plots • popular topics
For children who are ready to read on their own.

Reading Paragraphs   Grades 2–3
• challenging vocabulary • short paragraphs • exciting stories
For newly independent readers who read simple sentences with confidence.

Ready for Chapters   Grades 2–4
• chapters • longer paragraphs • full-color art
For children who want to take the plunge into chapter books but still like colorful pictures.

STEP INTO READING® is designed to give every child a successful reading experience. The grade levels are only guides; children will progress through the steps at their own speed, developing confidence in their reading. The F&P Text Level on the back cover serves as another tool to help you choose the right book for your child.

Remember, a lifetime love of reading starts with a single step!

For kids who have imaginary friends
—J.M.

Text copyright © 2017 by Julianne Moore
Cover art and interior illustrations copyright © 2017 by LeUyen Pham

Visit us on the Web!
StepIntoReading.com
randomhousekids.com

Educators and librarians, for a variety of teaching tools, visit us at RHTeachersLibrarians.com

Library of Congress Cataloging-in-Publication Data
Names: Moore, Julianne, author. | Pham, LeUyen, illustrator.
Title: Freckleface Strawberry : monster time! / by Julianne Moore ;
illustrated by LeUyen Pham.
Other titles: Monster time!
Description: New York : Random House, [2017] | Series: Step into reading.
Step 2 | Summary: Freckleface Strawberry must learn to compromise when no
one in the schoolyard wants to play monster with her.
Identifiers: LCCN 2016001145 (print) | LCCN 2016026307 (ebook) |
ISBN 978-0-385-39200-6 (pb) |
ISBN 978-0-375-97369-7 (hardcover library binding) |
ISBN 978-0-385-39202-0 (ebook)
Subjects: | CYAC: Play—Fiction. | Monsters—Fiction. | Recess—Fiction. |
Compromise (Ethics)—Fiction. | Schools—Fiction.
Classification: LCC PZ7.M78635 Frq 2017 (print) | LCC PZ7.M78635 (ebook) |
DDC [E]—dc23

Printed in the United States of America

10 9 8 7 6 5 4 3 2 1

This book has been officially leveled by using the F&P Text Level Gradient™ Leveling System.

FRECKLEFACE STRAWBERRY
Monster Time!

by Julianne Moore
illustrated by LeUyen Pham

Random House 🏠 New York

Freckleface Strawberry
cannot wait.
She cannot wait
for recess.

Because TODAY,
she wants
to play her game.
And everybody
will play with her.

Freckleface Strawberry
runs to the playground.

"Monster time!" she yells.
"I am a monster,
    and I am going to
    chase you!"

Winnie is playing
with chalk.
She is drawing
a picture of a house.

"Roar! I am a MONSTER!"
says Freckleface Strawberry.
"I am going to chase you!"

"No, thank you,"
says Winnie.
"I do not want
to be chased.
Do you want to draw?"

Freckleface Strawberry says,
"NO! I am a MONSTER!
IT IS MONSTER TIME!"
And Freckleface runs away.

Noah is playing
on the jungle gym.
He is hanging
upside down.

"Roar! I am a MONSTER!"
says Freckleface Strawberry.
"I am going to chase you!"

Noah says,
"Hang upside down
with me, Freckleface.
I do not want
to be chased
right now."

"NO!" says Freckleface.
"I AM A MONSTER!
IT IS MONSTER TIME!"
And she runs away.

Windy Pants Patrick
is playing ball.
He is bouncing the ball
up and down.

"ROAR!"

says Freckleface Strawberry.

"I AM A MONSTER,
AND I AM GOING TO
CHASE YOU!"

"I want to play ball,"
says Windy Pants.
"Will you play catch
with me?"
"NO!" says Freckleface.
"I AM GOING TO
CHASE YOU!"

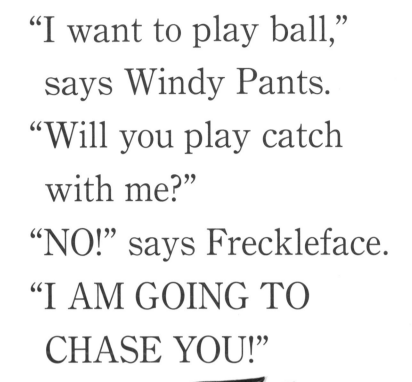

"NO!" says Windy Pants.
"Catch!"
"NO!" says Freckleface.
"MONSTER! IT IS ONLY
MONSTER TIME!!!!!!!!!!!!!"
And Freckleface runs away.

All the kids
are playing their games.
Windy Pants, Noah,
and Winnie draw a house.

They hang upside down
on the jungle gym.

And they play ball.

Freckleface Strawberry
is all alone.

"Roar," she says quietly.
"I am a monster,
and no one
will play with me."

Winnie sees Freckleface
and says,
"Freckleface,
do you want to draw?

"We can draw a monster."

Noah sees Freckleface
and says,
"Freckleface,
do you want to hang
upside down?

"We can play
upside-down monsters."

Windy Pants Patrick says, "How about a game of monster ball?"

So Freckleface Strawberry
plays with everybody.

And it is the best
monster time
of all.